James Lane Allen

Two Gentlemen of Kentucky

James Lane Allen

Two Gentlemen of Kentucky

ISBN/EAN: 9783743388567

Manufactured in Europe, USA, Canada, Australia, Japa

Cover: Foto ©Andreas Hilbeck / pixelio.de

Manufactured and distributed by brebook publishing software
(www.brebook.com)

James Lane Allen

Two Gentlemen of Kentucky

PETER

TWO GENTLEMEN
OF KENTUCKY

By
James Lane Allen

NEW YORK AND LONDON
HARPER & BROTHERS

MDCCCXCIX

Two Gentlemen of Kentucky

"The woods are hushed, their music is no more:
The leaf is dead, the yearning passed away:
New leaf, new life—the days of frost are o'er:
New life, new love, to suit the newer day."

THE WOODS ARE HUSHED

IT was near the middle of the afternoon of an autumnal day, on the wide, grassy plateau of Central Kentucky.

The Eternal Power seemed to have quitted the universe and left all nature folded in the calm of the Eternal Peace. Around the pale-blue dome of the heavens a few pearl-colored clouds hung motionless, as though the wind had been withdrawn to other skies. Not a crimson leaf floated downward through the soft, silvery light that

A   I

filled the atmosphere and created the sense of lonely, unimaginable spaces. This light overhung the far-rolling landscape of field and meadow and wood, crowning with faint radiance the remoter low-swelling hill-tops and deepening into dreamy half-shadows on their eastern slopes. Nearer, it fell in a white flake on an unstirred sheet of water which lay along the edge of a mass of sombre-hued woodland, and nearer still it touched to spring-like brilliancy a level, green meadow on the hither edge of the water, where a group of Durham cattle stood with reversed flanks near the gleaming trunks of some leafless syca-mores. Still nearer, it caught the top of the brown foliage of a little bent oak-tree and burned it into a silvery flame. It lit on the back and the wings of a crow flying heav-ily in the path of its rays, and made his blackness as white as the breast of a swan. In the immediate foreground, it sparkled in minute gleams along the stalks of the coarse, dead weeds that fell away from the legs and the flanks of a white horse, and slanted across the face of the rider and through the ends of his gray hair, which straggled from beneath his soft black hat.

The horse, old and patient and gentle, stood with low-stretched neck and closed eyes half asleep in the faint glow of the waning heat; and the rider, the sole human presence in all the field, sat looking across the silent autumnal landscape, sunk in reverie. Both horse and rider seemed but harmonious elements in the panorama of still-life, and completed the picture of a closing scene.

To the man it was a closing scene. From the rank, fallow field through which he had been riding he was now surveying, for the last time, the many features of a landscape that had been familiar to him from the beginning of memory. In the afternoon and the autumn of his age he was about to rend the last ties that bound him to his former life, and, like one who had survived his own destiny, turn his face towards a future that was void of everything he held significant or dear.

The Civil War had only the year before reached its ever-memorable close. From where he sat there was not a home in sight, as there was not one beyond the reach of his vision, but had felt its influence. Some of his neighbors had come home from its camps and prisons, aged or altered as though by half a lifetime of years. The bones of some lay whitening on its battle-fields. Families, reassembled around their hearth-stones, spoke in low tones unceasingly of defeat and victory, heroism and death. Suspicion

4

and distrust and estrangement pre-
vailed. Former friends met each
other on the turnpikes without
speaking; brothers avoided each
other in the streets of the neighboring town. The rich had grown
poor; the poor had become rich.
Many of the latter were preparing
to move West. The negroes were
drifting blindly hither and thither,
deserting the country and flocking
to the towns. Even the once united church of his neighborhood was
jarred by the unstrung and discord-
ant spirit of the times. At affect-
ing passages in the sermons men
grew pale and set their teeth fierce-
ly; women suddenly lowered their
black veils and rocked to and fro
in their pews; for it is always at
the bar of Conscience and before
the very altar of God that the human heart is most wrung by a sense
of its losses and the memory of its
wrongs. The war had divided the

people of Kentucky as the false mother would have severed the child.

It had not left the old man unscathed. His younger brother had fallen early in the conflict, borne to the end of his brief warfare by his impetuous valor; his aged mother had sunk under the tidings of the death of her latest-born; his sister was estranged from him by his political differences with her husband; his old family servants, men and women, had left him, and grass and weeds had already grown over the door-steps of the shut, noiseless cabins. Nay, the whole vast social system of the old régime had fallen, and he was henceforth but a useless fragment of the ruins.

All at once his mind turned from the cracked and smoky mirror of the times and dwelt fondly upon the scenes of the past. The silent fields around him seemed again alive with the negroes, singing as they followed the ploughs down the corn-rows or swung the cradles through the bearded wheat. Again, in a frenzy of merriment, the strains of the old fiddles issued from crevices of cabin-doors to the rhythmic beat of hands and feet that shook the rafters and the roof. Now he was sitting on his porch, and one little negro was blacking his shoes, another leading his saddle-horse to the stiles, a third bringing his hat, and a fourth handing him a glass of ice-cold sangaree; or now he lay under the locust-trees in his yard, falling asleep in the drowsy heat of the summer afternoon, while one waved over him a bough of pungent walnut leaves, until he lost consciousness, and by-and-by awoke to find that they both had fallen asleep side by side on the grass and that the abandoned fly-brush lay full across his face.

7

From where he sat also were seen slopes on which picnics were danced under the broad shade of maples and elms in June by those whom death and war had scattered like the transitory leaves that once had sheltered them. In this direction lay the district school-house where on Friday evenings there were wont to be speeches and debates; in that, lay the blacksmith's shop where of old he and his neighbors had met on horseback of Saturday afternoons to hear the news, get the mails, discuss elections, and pitch quoits. In the valley beyond stood the church at which all had assembled on calm Sunday mornings like the members of one united family. Along with these scenes went many a chastened reminiscence of bridal and funeral and simpler events that had made up the annals of his country life.

The reader will have a clearer insight into the character and past career of Colonel Romulus Fields by remembering that he represented a fair type of that social order which had existed in rank perfection over the blue-grass plains of Kentucky during the final decades of the old régime. Perhaps of all agriculturists in the United States the inhabitants of that region had spent the most nearly idyllic life, on account of the beauty of the climate, the richness of the land, the spacious comfort of their homes, the efficiency of their negroes, and the characteristic contentedness of their dispositions. Thus nature and history combined to make them a peculiar class, a cross between the aristocratic and the bucolic, being as simple as shepherds and as proud as kings, and not seldom exhibiting among both men and women types of character which were as remarkable for pure, tender, noble states of feeling as they were commonplace in powers and cultivation of mind.

It was upon this luxurious social growth that the war naturally fell as a killing frost, and upon no single specimen with more blighting power than upon Colonel Fields. For destiny had quarried and chiselled him, to serve as an ornament in the barbaric temple of human bondage. There *were* ornaments in that temple, and he was one. A slave-holder with Southern sympathies, a man educated not beyond the ideas of his generation, convinced that slavery was an evil, yet seeing no present way of removing it, he had of all things been a model master. As such he had gone on record in Kentucky, and no doubt in a Higher Court ; and as such his efforts had been put forth to secure the passage of many of those milder laws for which his State was distinguished. Often, in those dark days,

his face, anxious and sad, was to be
seen amid the throng that sur-
rounded the blocks on which slaves
were sold at auction; and more than
one poor wretch he had bought to
save him from separation from his
family or from being sold into the
Southern plantations — afterwards
riding far and near to find him a
home on one of the neighboring
farms.

But all those days were over.
He had but to place the whole picture of the present beside the whole
picture of the past to realize what
the contrast meant for him.

At length he gathered the bridle
reins from the neck of his old horse
and turned his head homeward. As
he rode slowly on, every spot gave
up its memories. He dismounted
when he came to the cattle and
walked among them, stroking their
soft flanks and feeling in the palm
of his hand the rasp of their salt-

loving tongues; on his sideboard at
home was many a silver cup which
told of premiums on cattle at the
great fairs. It was in this very
pond that as a boy he had learned
to swim on a cherry rail. When
he entered the woods, the sight of
the walnut-trees and the hickory-
nut trees, loaded on the topmost
branches, gave him a sudden pang.

Beyond the woods he came upon
the garden, which he had kept as
his mother had left it—an old-fashioned garden with an arbor in the
centre, covered with Isabella grape-
vines on one side and Catawba on
the other; with walks branching
thence in four directions, and along
them beds of jump-up-johnnies,
sweet-williams, daffodils, sweet-peas,
larkspur, and thyme, flags and the
sensitive-plant, celestial and maid-
en's-blush roses. He stopped and
looked over the fence at the very
spot where he had found his mother

on the day when the news of the battle came.

She had been kneeling, trowel in hand, driving away vigorously at the loamy earth, and, as she saw him coming, had risen and turned towards him her face with the ancient pink bloom on her clear cheeks and the light of a pure, strong soul in her gentle eyes. Overcome by his emotions, he had blindly faltered out the words, "Mother, John was among the killed!" For a moment she had looked at him as though stunned by a blow. Then a violent flush had overspread her features, and then an ashen pallor; after which, with a sudden proud dilating of her form as though with joy, she had sunk down like the tenderest of her lily-stalks cut from its root.

Beyond the garden he came to the empty cabin and the great wood-pile. At this hour it used to

13

be a scene of hilarious activity—the little negroes sitting perched in chattering groups on the topmost logs or playing leap-frog in the dust, while some picked up baskets of chips or dragged a back-log into the cabins.

At last he drew near the wooden stiles and saw the large house of which he was the solitary occupant. What darkened rooms and noiseless halls! What beds, all ready, that nobody now came to sleep in, and cushioned old chairs that nobody rocked! The house and the contents of its attic, presses, and drawers could have told much of the history of Kentucky from almost its beginning; for its foundations had been laid by his father near the beginning of the century, and through its doors had passed a long train of forms, from the veterans of the Revolution to the soldiers of the Civil War. Old coats hung up in closets; old dresses

14

folded away in drawers; saddle-
bags and buckskin leggings; hunt-
ing-jackets, powder-horns, and
militiamen hats; looms and knit-
ting-needles; snuff-boxes and reti-
cules — what a treasure-house of
the past it was! And now the only
thing that had the springs of life
within its bosom was the great,
sweet-voiced clock, whose faithful
face had kept unchanged amid all
the swift pageantry of changes.

He dismounted at the stiles and
handed the reins to a gray-haired
negro, who had hobbled up to receive them with a smile and a gest-
ure of the deepest respect.

" Peter," he said, very simply, " I
am going to sell the place and move
to town. I can't live here any
longer."

With these words he passed
through the yard-gate, walked slowly up the broad pavement, and entered the house.

15

ON the disappearing form of the colonel was fixed an ancient pair of eyes that looked out at him from behind a still more ancient pair of silver-rimmed spectacles with an expression of indescribable solicitude and love.

These eyes were set in the head of an old gentleman—for such he was—named Peter Cotton, who was the only one of the colonel's former slaves that had remained inseparable from his person and his altered fortunes. In early manhood Peter had been a wood-chopper; but he had one day had his leg broken by the limb of a falling tree, and afterwards, out of consideration for his limp, had been made supervisor of the wood-pile, gardener, and a sort of nondescript servitor of his master's luxurious needs.

Nay, in larger and deeper characters must his history be writ, he having been, in days gone by, one of those ministers of the gospel whom conscientious Kentucky masters often urged to the exercise of spiritual functions in behalf of their benighted people. In course of preparation for this august work, Peter had learned to read, and had come to possess a well-chosen library of three several volumes—*Webster's Spelling-book, The Pilgrim's Progress,* and the Bible. But even these unusual acquisitions he deemed not enough; for being touched with a spark of poetic fire from heaven, and fired by the African's fondness for all that is conspicuous in dress, he had conceived for himself the creation of a unique garment which should symbolize in perfection the claims and consolations of his apostolic office. This was nothing less than a sacred blue-jeans coat that he had had his old mistress make him, with very long and spacious tails, whereon, at his further direction, she embroidered sundry texts of Scripture which it pleased him to regard as the fit visible annunciations of his holy calling. And inasmuch as his mistress, who had had the coat woven on her own looms from the wool of her finest sheep, was, like other gentlewomen of her time, rarely skilled in the accomplishments of the needle, and was moreover in full sympathy with the piety of his intent, she wrought of these passages a border enriched with such intricate curves, marvellous flourishes, and harmonious letterings, that Solomon never reflected the glory in which Peter was arrayed whenever he put it on. For after much prayer that the Almighty

wisdom would aid his reason in the
difficult task of selecting the most
appropriate texts, Peter had chosen
seven—one for each day in the week
—with such tact, and no doubt
heavenly guidance, that when braid-
ed together they did truly constitute
an eloquent epitome of Christian
duty, hope, and pleading.

From first to last they were as
follows: "Woe is unto me if I
preach not the gospel;" "Servants,
be obedient to them that are your
masters according to the flesh;"
"Come unto me, all ye that labour
and are heavy laden;" "Consider
the lilies of the field, how they grow;
they toil not, neither do they spin;"
"Now abideth faith, hope, and
charity, these three; but the greatest
of these is charity;" "I would not
have you to be ignorant, brethren,
concerning them which are asleep;"
"For as in Adam all die, even so in
Christ shall all be made alive." This

concatenation of texts Peter wished
to have duly solemnized, and therefore, when the work was finished, he
further requested his mistress to
close the entire chain with the word
"Amen," introduced in some suit-
able place.

But the only spot now left vacant
was one of a few square inches,
located just where the coat-tails
hung over the end of Peter's spine;
so that when any one stood full in
Peter's rear, he could but marvel at
the sight of so solemn a word em-
blazoned in so unusual a locality.

Panoplied in this robe of right-
eousness, and with a worn leathern
Bible in his hand, Peter used to go
around of Sundays, and during the
week by night, preaching from
cabin to cabin the gospel of his
heavenly Master.

The angriest lightnings of the
sultriest skies often played amid the
darkness upon those sacred coat-tails

and around that girdle of everlast-
ing texts, as though the evil spirits
of the air would fain have burned
them and scattered their ashes on
the roaring winds. The slow-sifting
snows of winter whitened them as
though to chill their spiritual fires;
but winter and summer, year after
year, in weariness of body, often in
sore distress of mind, for miles along
this lonely road and for miles across
that rugged way, Peter trudged on
and on, withal perhaps as meek a
spirit as ever grew foot-sore in the
paths of its Master. Many a poor
overburdened slave took fresh heart
and strength from the sight of that
celestial raiment; many a stubborn,
rebellious spirit, whose flesh but
lately quivered under the lash, was
brought low by its humble teaching;
many a worn-out old frame, racked
with pain in its last illness, pressed
a fevered lip to its hopeful hem;
and many a dying eye closed in

death peacefully fixed on its immortal pledges.

When Peter started abroad, if a storm threatened, he carried an old cotton umbrella of immense size; and as the storm burst, he gathered the tails of his coat carefully up under his armpits that they might be kept dry. Or if caught by a tempest without his umbrella, he would take his coat off and roll it up inside out, leaving his body exposed to the fury of the elements. No care, however, could keep it from growing old and worn and faded; and when the slaves were set free and he was called upon by the interposition of Providence to lay it finally aside, it was covered by many a patch and stain as proofs of its devoted usage.

One after another the colonel's old servants, gathering their children about them, had left him, to begin their new life. He bade them all a kind good-by, and into the palm of each silently pressed some gift that he knew would soon be needed. But no inducement could make Peter or Phillis, his wife, budge from their cabin. " Go, Peter! Go, Phillis !" the colonel had said time and again. " No one is happier that you are free than I am ; and you can call on me for what you need to set you up in business." But Peter and Phillis asked to stay with him. Then suddenly, several months before the time at which this sketch opens, Phillis had died, leaving the colonel and Peter as the only relics of that populous life which had once filled the house and the cabins. The colonel had succeeded in hiring a woman to do Phillis's work; but her presence was a strange note of discord in the old domestic harmony, and only saddened the recollections of its vanished peace.

Peter had a short, stout figure, dark - brown skin, smooth - shaven face, eyes round, deep-set, and wide apart, and a short stub nose which dipped suddenly into his head, making it easy for him to wear the silver-rimmed spectacles left him by his old mistress. A peculiar conformation of the muscles between the eyes and the nose gave him the quizzical expression of one who is about to sneeze, and this was heightened by a twinkle in the eyes which seemed caught from the shining of an inner sun upon his tranquil heart.

Sometimes, however, his face grew sad enough. It was sad on this afternoon while he watched the colonel walk slowly up the pavement, well overgrown with weeds, and enter the house, which the setting sun touched with the last radiance of the finished day.

24

ABOUT two years after the close of the war, therefore, the colonel and Peter were to be found in Lexington, ready to turn over a new leaf in the volumes of their lives, which already had an old-fashioned binding, a somewhat musty odor, and but few unwritten leaves remaining.

After a long, dry summer you may have seen two gnarled old apple-trees, that stood with interlocked arms on the western slope of some quiet hill-side, make a melancholy show of blooming out again in the autumn of the year and dallying with the idle buds that mock their sapless branches. Much the same was the belated, fruitless efflorescence of the colonel and Peter.

25

The colonel had no business habits, no political ambition, no wish to grow richer. He was too old for society, and without near family ties. For some time he wandered through the streets like one lost—sick with yearning for the fields and woods, for his cattle, for familiar faces. He haunted Cheapside and the court-house square, where the farmers always assembled when they came to town; and if his eye lighted on one, he would button-hole him on the street-corner and lead him into a grocery and sit down for a quiet chat. Sometimes he would meet an aimless, melancholy wanderer like himself, and the two would go off and discuss over and over again their departed days; and several times he came unexpectedly upon some of his old servants who had fallen into bitter want, and who more than repaid him for the help he gave by contrasting the hardships of a life of freedom with the ease of their shackled years.

In the course of time, he could but observe that human life in the town was reshaping itself slowly and painfully, but with resolute energy. The colossal structure of slavery had fallen, scattering its ruins far and wide over the State ; but out of the very débris was being taken the material to lay the deeper foundations of the new social edifice. Men and women as old as he were beginning life over, and trying to fit themselves for it by changing the whole attitude and habit of their minds—by taking on a new heart and spirit. But when a great building falls, there is always some rubbish, and the colonel and others like him were part of this. Henceforth they possessed only an antiquarian sort of interest, like the stamped bricks of Nebuchadnezzar.

Nevertheless he made a show of

doing something, and in a year or two opened on Cheapside a store for the sale of hardware and agricultural implements. He knew more about the latter than anything else; and, furthermore, he secretly felt that a business of this kind would enable him to establish in town a kind of headquarters for the farmers. His account-books were to be kept on a system of twelve months' credit; and he resolved that if one of his customers couldn't pay then, it would make no difference.

Business began slowly. The farmers dropped in and found a good lounging-place. On county-court days, which were great market-days for the sale of sheep, horses, mules, and cattle in front of the colonel's door, they swarmed in from the hot sun and sat around on the counter and the ploughs and machines till the entrance was blocked to other customers.

28

When a customer did come in, the colonel, who was probably talking with some old acquaintance, would tell him just to look around and pick out what he wanted and the price would be all right. If one of those acquaintances asked for a pound of nails, the colonel would scoop up some ten pounds and say, "I reckon that's about a pound, Tom." He had never seen a pound of nails in his life; and if one had been weighed on his scales, he would have said the scales were wrong.

He had no great idea of commercial despatch. One morning a lady came in for some carpet-tacks, an article that he had forgotten to lay in. But he at once sent off an order for enough to have tacked a carpet pretty well all over Kentucky; and when they came, two weeks later, he told Peter to take her up a dozen papers with his compliments.

He had laid in, however, an ample
and especially fine assortment of
pocket-knives, for that instrument
had always been to him one of gracious and very winning qualities.
Then when a friend dropped in he
would say, "General, don't you need
a new pocket-knife?" and, taking
out one, would open all the blades
and commend the metal and the
handle. The "general" would in-
quire the price, and the colonel,
having shut the blades, would hand
it to him, saying in a careless, fond
way, "I reckon I won't charge you
anything for that." His mind could
not come down to the low level of
such ignoble barter, and he gave
away the whole case of knives.

These were the pleasanter aspects
of his business life, which did not
lack as well its tedium and crosses.
Thus there were many dark stormy
days when no one he cared to see
came in; and he then became rather

a pathetic figure, wandering absently around amid the symbols of his past activity, and stroking the ploughs, like dumb companions. Or he would stand at the door and look across at the old court - house, where he had seen many a slave sold and had listened to the great Kentucky orators.

But what hurt him most was the talk of the new farming and the abuse of the old which he was forced to hear; and he generally refused to handle the improved implements and mechanical devices by which labor and waste were to be saved.

Altogether he grew tired of "the thing," and sold out at the end of the year with a loss of over a thousand dollars, though he insisted he had done a good business.

As he was then seen much on the streets again and several times heard to make remarks in regard to the sidewalks, gutters, and crossings,

31

when they happened to be in bad condition, the *Daily Press* one morning published a card stating that if Colonel Romulus Fields would consent to make the race for mayor he would receive the support of many Democrats, adding a tribute to his virtues and his influential past. It touched the colonel, and he walked down-town with a rather commanding figure the next morning. But it pained him to see how many of his acquaintances returned his salutations very coldly; and just as he was passing the Northern Bank he met the young opposition candidate —a little red-haired fellow, walking between two ladies, with a rose-bud in his button-hole—who refused to speak at all, but made the ladies laugh by some remark he uttered as the colonel passed. The card had been inserted humorously, but he took it seriously; and when his friends found this out, they rallied round him. The day of election drew near. They told him he must buy votes. He said he wouldn't buy a vote to be mayor of the New Jerusalem. They told him he must "mix" and "treat." He refused. Foreseeing he had no chance, they besought him to withdraw. He said he would not. They told him he wouldn't poll twenty votes. He replied that *one* would satisfy him, provided it was neither begged nor bought. When his defeat was announced, he accepted it as another evidence that he had no part in the present—no chance of redeeming his idleness.

A sense of this weighed heavily on him at times; but it is not likely that he realized how pitifully he was undergoing a moral shrinkage in consequence of mere disuse. Actually, extinction had set in with him long prior to dissolution, and he was dead years before his heart

C   33

ceased beating. The very basic virtues on which had rested his once
spacious and stately character were
now but the mouldy corner-stones
of a crumbling ruin.

It was a subtle evidence of dete-
rioration in manliness that he had
taken to dress. When he had lived
in the country, he had never dressed
up unless he came to town. When
he had moved to town, he thought
he must remain dressed up all the
time; and this fact first fixed his
attention on a matter which afterwards began to be loved for its
own sake. Usually he wore a Der-
by hat, a black diagonal coat, gray
trousers, and a white necktie. But
the article of attire in which he took
chief pleasure was hose; and the
better to show the gay colors of
these, he wore low-cut shoes of the
finest calf-skin, turned up at the
toes. Thus his feet kept pace with
the present, however far his head

may have lagged in the past ; and it may be that this stream of fresh fashions, flowing perennially over his lower extremities like water about the roots of a tree, kept him from drying up altogether.

Peter always polished his shoes with too much blacking, perhaps thinking that the more the blacking the greater the proof of love. He wore his clothes about a season and a half—having several suits —and then passed them on to Peter, who, foreseeing the joy of such an inheritance, bought no new ones. In the act of transferring them the colonel made no comment until he came to the hose, from which he seemed unable to part without a final tribute of esteem, as : "These are fine, Peter ;" or, " Peter, these are nearly as good as new." Thus Peter, too, was dragged through the whims of fashion. To have seen the colonel walking about his

35

grounds and garden followed by Peter, just a year and a half behind in dress and a yard and a half behind in space, one might well have taken the rear figure for the colonel's double, slightly the worse for wear, somewhat shrunken, and cast into a heavy shadow.

Time hung so heavily on his hands at night that with a happy inspiration he added a dress-suit to his wardrobe, and accepted the first invitation to an evening party.

He grew excited as the hour approached, and dressed in a great fidget for fear he should be too late.

"How do I look, Peter?" he inquired at length, surprised at his own appearance.

"Splendid, Marse Rom," replied Peter, bringing in the shoes with more blacking on them than ever before.

"I think," said the colonel, apologetically—"I think I'd look bet-

ter if I'd put a little powder on. I
don't know what makes me so red
in the face."

But his heart began to sink before he reached his hostess's, and he
had a fearful sense of being the ob-
served of all observers as he slipped
through the hall and passed rapidly
up to the gentlemen's room. He
stayed there after the others had
gone down, bewildered and lonely,
dreading to go down himself. By-
and-by the musicians struck up a
waltz, and with a little cracked
laugh at his own performance he cut
a few shines of an unremembered
pattern; but his ankles snapped
audibly, and he suddenly stopped
with the thought of what Peter
would say if he should catch him
at these antics. Then he boldly
went down-stairs.

He had touched the new human
life around him at various points:
as he now stretched out his arms

towards its society, for the first time
he completely realized how far re-
moved it was from him. Here he
saw a younger generation — the
flowers of the new social order —
sprung from the very soil of frater-
nal battle - fields, but blooming together as the emblems of oblivious
peace. He saw fathers who had
fought madly on opposite sides
talking quietly in corners as they
watched their children dancing, or
heard them toasting their old gen-
erals and their campaigns over their
champagne in the supper-room. He
was glad of it; but it made him feel,
at the same time, that instead of
treading the velvety floors, he ought
to step up and take his place among
the canvases of old - time portraits
that looked down from the walls.

The dancing he had done had
been not under the blinding glare
of gas-light, but by the glimmer of
tallow-dips and star-candles and the

ruddy glow of cavernous firesides—
not to the accompaniment of an or-
chestra of wind-instruments and
strings, but to a chorus of girls'
sweet voices, as they trod simpler
measures, or to the maddening
sway of a gray-haired negro fiddler
standing on a chair in the chimney-
corner. Still, it is significant to note
that his saddest thought, long after
leaving, was that his shirt-bosom
had not lain down smooth, but
stuck out like a huge cracked egg-
shell; and that when, in imitation
of the others, he had laid his white
silk handkerchief across his bosom
inside his vest, it had slipped out
during the evening, and had been
found by him, on confronting a mirror, flapping over his stomach like
a little white masonic apron.

"Did you have a nice time, Marse
Rom?" inquired Peter, as they drove
home through the darkness.

"Splendid time, Peter, splendid

time," replied the colonel, nervously.

"Did you dance any, Marse Rom?"

"I didn't *dance*. Oh, I *could* have danced if I'd *wanted* to; but I didn't."

Peter helped the colonel out of the carriage with pitying gentleness when they reached home. It was the first and only party.

Peter also had been finding out that his occupation was gone.

Soon after moving to town, he had tendered his pastoral services to one of the fashionable churches of the city—not because it was fashionable, but because it was made up of his brethren. In reply he was invited to preach a trial sermon, which he did with gracious unction.

It was a strange scene, as one calm Sunday morning he stood on the edge of the pulpit, dressed in a suit of the colonel's old clothes, with one hand in his trousers-pocket, and his lame leg set a little forward at an angle familiar to those who know the statues of Henry Clay.

How self-possessed he seemed, yet with what a rush of memories did he pass his eyes slowly over that vast assemblage of his emancipated people! With what feelings must he have contrasted those silk hats, and walking-canes, and broadcloths; those gloves and satins, laces and feathers, jewelry and fans—that whole many-colored panorama of life — with the weary, sad, and sullen audiences that had often heard him of old under the forest trees or by the banks of some turbulent stream!

In a voice husky, but heard beyond the flirtation of the uttermost pew, he took his text: "Consider the lilies of the field, how they

41

grow; they toil not, neither do they spin." From this he tried to preach a new sermon, suited to the newer day. But several times the thoughts of the past were too much for him, and he broke down with emotion.

The next day a grave committee waited on him and reported that the sense of the congregation was to call a colored gentleman from Louisville. Private objections to Peter were that he had a broken leg, wore Colonel Fields's second-hand clothes, which were too big for him, preached in the old-fashioned way, and lacked self-control and repose of manner.

Peter accepted his rebuff as sweetly as Socrates might have done. Humming the burden of an old hymn, he took his righteous coat from a nail in the wall and folded it away in a little brass-nailed deer-skin trunk, laying over

42

it the spelling-book and the *Pilgrim's Progress*, which he had ceased to read. Thenceforth his relations to his people were never intimate, and even from the other servants of the colonel's household he stood apart. But the colonel took Peter's rejection greatly to heart, and the next morning gave him the new silk socks he had worn at the party. In paying his servants the colonel would sometimes say, "Peter, I reckon I'd better begin to pay you a salary; that's the style now." But Peter would turn off, saying he didn't "have no use fur no salary."

Thus both of them dropped more and more out of life, but as they did so drew more and more closely to each other. The colonel had bought a home on the edge of the town, with some ten acres of beautiful ground surrounding. A high osage-orange hedge shut it in, and forest trees, chiefly maples and elms, gave to the lawn and house abundant shade. Wild-grape vines, the Virginia-creeper, and the climbing-oak swung their long festoons from summit to summit, while honey-suckles, clematis, and the Mexican-vine clambered over arbors and trellises, or along the chipped stone of the low, old-fashioned house. Just outside the door of the colonel's bedroom slept an ancient, broken sun-dial.

The place seemed always in half-shadow, with hedgerows of box, clumps of dark holly, darker firs half a century old, and aged crape-like cedars.

It was in the seclusion of this retreat, which looked almost like a wild bit of country set down on the edge of the town, that the colonel and Peter spent more of their time as they fell farther in the rear of onward events. There were no such flower-gardens in the city, and pretty much the whole town went thither for its flowers, preferring them to those that were to be had for a price at the nurseries.

There was, perhaps, a suggestion of pathetic humor in the fact that it should have called on the colonel and Peter, themselves so nearly defunct, to furnish the flowers for so many funerals; but, it is certain, almost weekly the two old gentlemen received this chastening admonition of their all-but-spent mortality. The colonel cultivated the rarest fruits also, and had under glass varieties that were not friendly to the climate; so that by means of the fruits and flowers there was established a pleasant social bond with many who otherwise would never have sought them out.

But others came for better reasons. To a few deep-seeing eyes the colonel and Peter were ruined landmarks on a fading historic landscape, and their devoted friendship was the last

steady burning-down of that pure
flame of love which can never again
shine out in the future of the two
races. Hence a softened charm in-
vested the drowsy quietude of that
shadowy paradise in which the old
master without a slave and the old
slave without a master still kept up
a brave pantomime of their obsolete
relations. No one ever saw in their
intercourse ought but the finest
courtesy, the most delicate consideration. The very tones of their
voices in addressing each other were
as good as sermons on gentleness,
their antiquated playfulness as melo-
dious as the babble of distant water.
To be near them was to be exorcised
of evil passions.

The sun of their day had indeed
long since set; but like twin clouds
lifted high and motionless into some
far quarter of the gray twilight skies,
they were still radiant with the glow
of the invisible orb.

Henceforth the colonel's appearances in public were few and regular. He went to church on Sundays, where he sat on the edge of the choir in the centre of the building, and sang an ancient bass of his own improvisation to the older hymns, and glanced furtively around to see whether any one noticed that he could not sing the new ones. At the Sunday-school picnics the committee of arrangements allowed him to carve the mutton, and after dinner to swing the smallest children gently beneath the trees. He was seen on Commencement Day at Morrison Chapel, where he always gave his bouquet to the valedictorian. It was the speech of that young gentleman that always touched him, consisting as it did of farewells.

In the autumn he might sometimes be noticed sitting high up in the amphitheatre at the fair, a little blue around the nose, and looking

absently over into the ring where
the judges were grouped around the
music-stand. Once he had strutted
around as a judge himself, with a
blue ribbon in his button-hole, while
the band played "Sweet Alice, Ben
Bolt" and "Gentle Annie." The
ring seemed full of young men now,
and no one even thought of offering
him the privileges of the grounds.
In his day the great feature of the
exhibition had been cattle; now
everything was turned into a horse-
show. He was always glad to get
home again to Peter, his true yoke-
fellow. For just as two old oxen—
one white and one black—that have
long toiled under the same yoke will,
when turned out to graze at last in
the widest pasture, come and put
themselves horn to horn and flank
to flank, so the colonel and Peter
were never so happy as when rumi-
nating side by side.

IN their eventless life the slightest
incident acquired the importance of
a history. Thus, one day in June,
Peter discovered a young couple
love-making in the shrubbery, and
with the deepest agitation reported
the fact to the colonel.

Never before, probably, had the
fluttering of the dear god's wings
brought more dismay than to these
ancient involuntary guardsmen of
his hiding-place. The colonel was
at first for breaking up what he
considered a piece of underhand
proceedings, but Peter reasoned
stoutly that if the pair were driven
out they would simply go to some
other retreat; and without getting
the approval of his conscience to

D   49

this view, the colonel contented himself with merely repeating that they ought to go straight and tell the girl's parents. Those parents lived just across the street outside his grounds. The young lady he knew very well himself, having a few years before given her the privilege of making herself at home among his flowers. It certainly looked hard to drive her out now, just when she was making the best possible use of his kindness and her opportunity. Moreover, Peter walked down street and ascertained that the young fellow was an energetic farmer living a few miles from town, and son of one of the colonel's former friends; on both of which accounts the latter's heart went out to him. So when, a few days later, the colonel, followed by Peter, crept up breathlessly and peeped through the bushes at the pair strolling along the shady perfumed walks, and so plainly happy in that happiness which comes but once in a lifetime, they not only abandoned the idea of betraying the secret, but afterwards kept away from that part of the grounds, lest they should be an interruption.

"Peter," stammered the colonel, who had been trying to get the words out for three days, "do you suppose he has already—*asked* her?"

"Some's pow'ful quick on de trigger, en some's mighty slow," replied Peter, neutrally. "En some," he added, exhaustively, "don't use de trigger 't all!"

"I always thought there had to be asking done by *somebody*," remarked the colonel, a little vaguely.

"I nuver axed Phillis!" exclaimed Peter, with a certain air of triumph.

"Did Phillis ask *you*, Peter?" inquired the colonel, blushing and confidential.

"No, no, Marse Rom! I couldn't er stood dat from no 'oman!" replied

Peter, laughing, and shaking his head.

The colonel was sitting on the stone steps in front of the house, and Peter stood below, leaning against a Corinthian column, hat in hand, as he went on to tell his love-story.

"Hit all happ'n dis way, Marse Rom. We wuz gwine have pra'r-meetin', en I 'lowed to walk home wid Phillis en ax 'er on de road. I been 'lowin' to ax 'er heap o' times befo', but I ain' jes nuver done so. So I says to myse'f, says I, 'I jes mek my sermon to-night kiner lead up to whut I gwine tell Phillis on de road home.' So I tuk my tex' from de *lef'* tail o' my coat: 'De greates' o' dese is charity'; caze I knowed charity wuz same ez love. En all de time I wuz preachin' an' glorifyin' charity en identifyin' charity wid love, I couldn' he'p thinkin' 'bout what I gwine say to

52

Phillis on de road home. Dat mek me feel better; en de better I *feel*, de better I *preach*, so hit boun' to mek my *heahehs* feel better likewise —Phillis 'mong um. So Phillis she jes sot dah listenin' en listenin' en lookin' like we wuz a'ready on de road home, till I got so wuked up in my feelin's I jes knowed de time wuz come. By-en-by, I had n' mo' 'n done preachin' en wuz lookin' roun' to git my Bible en my hat, 'fo' up popped dat big Charity Green, who been settin' 'longside o' Phillis en tekin' ev'y las' thing I said to *her*- se'f. En she tuk hole o' my han' en squeeze it, en say she felt mos' like shoutin'. En 'fo' I knowed it, I jes see Phillis wrap 'er shawl roun' 'er head en tu'n 'er nose up at me right quick en flip out de dooh. De dogs howl mighty mou'nful when I walk home by myse'f *dat* night," added Peter, laughing to himself, " en I ain' preach dat sermon no mo' tell atter me en Phillis wuz married.

" Hit was long time," he contin- ued, " 'fo' Phillis come to heah me preach any mo'. But 'long 'bout de nex' fall we had big meetin', en heap mo' um j'ined. But Phillis, she ain't nuver j'ined yit. I preached mighty nigh all roun' my coat-tails till I say to myse'f, D' ain't but one tex' lef', en I jes got to fetch 'er wid dat! De tex' wuz on de *right* tail o' my coat: 'Come unto me, all ye dat labor en is heavy laden.' Hit wuz a ve'y momentous sermon, en all 'long I jes see Phillis wras'lin' wid 'erse'f, en I say, 'She *got* to come *dis* night, de Lohd he'pin' me.' En I had n' mo' 'n said de word, 'fo' she jes walked down en guv me 'er han'.

" Den we had de baptizin' in Elk- horn Creek, en de watter wuz deep en de curren' tol'ble swif'. Hit look to me like dere wuz five hundred

uv um on de creek side. By-en-by
I stood on de edge o' de watter, en
Phillis she come down to let me
baptize 'er. En me en 'er j'ined
han's en waded out in the creek,
mighty slow, caze Phillis didn' have
no shot roun' de bottom uv 'er
dress, en it kep' bobbin' on top de
watter till I pushed it down. But
by-en-by we got 'way out in de
creek, en bof uv us wuz tremblin'.
En I says to 'er ve'y kin'ly, ' When
I put you un'er de watter, Phillis,
you mus' try en hole yo'se'f stiff, so
I can lif' you up easy.' But I hadn't
mo' 'n jes got 'er laid back over de
watter ready to souze 'er un'er
when 'er feet flew up off de bottom
uv de creek, en when I retched out
to fetch 'er up, I stepped in a hole ;
en 'fo' I knowed it we wuz floun-
derin' roun' in de watter, en de
hymn dey was singin' on de bank
sounded mighty confused-like. En
Phillis she swallowed some watter,

en all 't oncet she jes grap me right tight roun' de neck, en say mighty quick, says she, 'I gwine marry whoever gits me out'n dis yere watter!'

"En by-en-by, when me en 'er wuz walkin' up de bank o' de creek, drippin' all over, I says to 'er, says I :

"'Does you 'member what you said back yon'er in de watter, Phillis?'

"'I ain' out'n no watter yit,' says she, ve'y contemptuous.

"'When does you consider yo'-se'f out'n de watter?' says I, ve'y humble.

"'When I git dese soakin' clo'es off'n my back,' says she.

"Hit wuz good dark when we got home, en atter a while I crope up to de dooh o' Phillis's cabin en put my eye down to de key-hole, en see Phillis jes settin' 'fo' dem blazin' walnut logs dressed up in 'er new red linsey dress, en 'er eyes shinin'. En I shuk so I 'mos' faint. Den I tap easy on de dooh, en say in a mighty tremblin' tone, says I :

"'Is you out'n de watter yit, Phillis?'

"'I got on dry dress,' says she.

"'Does you 'member what you said back yon'er in de watter, Phillis?' says I.

"'De latch-string on de outside de dooh,' says she, mighty sof'.

"En I walked in."

As Peter drew near the end of this reminiscence, his voice sank to a key of inimitable tenderness; and when it was ended he stood a few minutes, scraping the gravel with the toe of his boot, his head dropped forward. Then he added, huskily:

"Phillis been dead heap o' years now;" and turned away.

This recalling of the scenes of a time long gone by may have awakened in the breast of the colonel some gentle memory; for after Peter was gone he continued to sit a while in silent musing. Then, getting up, he walked in the falling twilight across the yard and through the gardens until he came to a secluded spot in the most distant corner. There he stooped, or rather knelt, down and passed his hands, as though with mute benediction, over a little bed of old-fashioned China pinks. When he had moved in from the country he had brought nothing away from his mother's garden but these, and in all the years since no one had ever pulled them, as Peter well knew; for one day the colonel had said, with his face turned away:

"Let them have all the flowers they want; but leave the pinks."

He continued kneeling over them now, touching them softly with his fingers, as though they were the fragrant, never-changing symbols of voiceless communion with his past. Still, it may have been only the early dew of the evening that glistened on them when he rose and slowly walked away, leaving the pale moonbeams to haunt the spot.

Certainly after this day he showed increasing concern in the young lovers who were holding clandestine meetings in his grounds.

"Peter," he would say, "why, if they love each other, don't they get married? Something may happen."

"I been spectin' some'n' to happ'n fur some time, ez dey been quar'lin' right smart lately," replied Peter, laughing.

Whether or not he was justified in this prediction, before the end of another week the colonel read a notice of their elopement and marriage; and several days later he came up from down-town and told Peter that everything had been forgiven the young pair, who had gone to house-keeping in the country. It gave him pleasure to think he had helped to perpetuate the race of blue-grass farmers.

IT was in the twilight of a late autumn day in the same year that nature gave the colonel the first direct intimation to prepare for the last summons. They had been passing along the garden walks, where a few pale flowers were trying to flourish up to the very winter's edge, and where the dry leaves had gathered unswept and rustled beneath their feet. All at once the colonel turned to Peter, who was a yard and a half behind, as usual, and said:

"Give me your arm, Peter, I feel tired;" and thus the two, for the first time in all their lifetime walking abreast, passed slowly on.

"Peter," said the colonel, gravely, a minute or two later, "we are like

61

two dried-up stalks of fodder. I wonder the Lord lets us live any longer."

"I reck'n He's managin' to use us *some* way, or we wouldn' be heah," said Peter.

"Well, all I have to say is that, if He's using me, He can't be in much of a hurry for his work," replied the colonel.

"He uses snails, en I *know* we ain' ez slow ez *dem*," argued Peter, composedly.

"I don't know. I think a snail must have made more progress since the war than I have."

The idea of his uselessness seemed to weigh on him, for a little later he remarked, with a sort of mortified smile :

"Do you think, Peter, that we would pass for what they call representative men of the New South?"

"We done *had* ou' day, Marse Rom," replied Peter. "We got to pass fur what we *wuz*. Mebbe de *Lohd's* got mo' use fur us yit 'n *people* has," he added, after a pause.

From this time on the colonel's strength gradually failed him ; but it was not until the following spring that the end came.

A night or two before his death his mind wandered backward, after the familiar manner of the dying, and his delirious dreams showed the shifting, faded pictures that renewed themselves for the last time on his wasting memory. It must have been that he was once more amid the scenes of his active farm-life, for his broken snatches of talk ran thus:

"Come, boys, get your cradles! Look where the sun is! You are late getting to work this morning. That is the finest field of wheat in the county. Be careful about the bundles! Make them the same size and tie them tight. That swath is

too wide, and you don't hold your
cradle right, Tom. . . .

"Sell *Peter!* Sell *Peter Cotton!*
No, sir! You might buy *me* some
day and work *me* in your cotton-
field; but as long as he's mine, you
can't buy Peter, and you can't buy
any of *my* negroes. . . .

"Boys! boys! If you don't work
faster, you won't finish this field to-
day. . . . You'd better go in the
shade and rest now. The sun's very
hot. Don't drink too much ice-
water. There's a jug of whiskey in
the fence-corner. Give them a good
dram around, and tell them to work
slow till the sun gets lower.". . .

Once during the night a sweet
smile played over his features as he
repeated a few words that were part
of an·old rustic song and dance.
Arranged, not as they came broken
and incoherent from his lips, but as
he once had sung them, they were
as follows:

" O Sister Phœbe ! How merry were we
When we sat under the juniper-tree,
    The juniper-tree, heigh-ho !
Put this hat on your head ! Keep your
  head warm ;
Take a sweet kiss ! It will do you no harm,
    Do you no harm, I know !"

After this he sank into a quieter sleep, but soon stirred with a look of intense pain.

"Helen ! Helen !" he murmured. "Will you break your promise? Have you changed in your feelings towards me? I have brought you the pinks. Won't you take the pinks, Helen ?"

Then he sighed as he added, " It wasn't her fault. If she had only known—"

Who was the Helen of that far-away time? Was this the colonel's love-story ?

But during all the night, whithersoever his mind wandered, at intervals it returned to the burden of a single strain—the harvesting. Towards daybreak he took it up again for the last time :

"O boys, boys, *boys!* If you don't work faster you won't finish the field to-day. Look how low the sun is! . . . I am going to the house. They can't finish the field to-day. Let them do what they can, but don't let them work late. I want Peter to go to the house with me. Tell him to come on.". . .

In the faint gray of the morning, Peter, who had been watching by the bedside all night, stole out of the room, and going into the garden pulled a handful of pinks—a thing he had never done before—and, re-entering the colonel's bedroom, put them in a vase near his sleeping face. Soon afterwards the colonel opened his eyes and looked around him. At the foot of the bed stood Peter, and on one side sat the physician and a friend. The night-lamp burned low, and through the folds of the curtains came the white light of early day.

"Put out the lamp and open the curtains," he said, feebly. "It's day." When they had drawn the curtains aside, his eyes fell on the pinks, sweet and fresh with the dew on them. He stretched out his hand and touched them caressingly, and his eyes sought Peter's with a look of grateful understanding.

"I want to be alone with Peter for a while," he said, turning his face towards the others.

When they were left alone, it was some minutes before anything was said. Peter, not knowing what he did, but knowing what was coming, had gone to the window and hid himself behind the curtains, drawing them tightly around his form as though to shroud himself from sorrow.

At length the colonel said, "Come here!"

Peter, almost staggering forward, fell at the foot of the bed, and, clasping the colonel's feet with one arm, pressed his cheek against them.

"Come closer!"

Peter crept on his knees and buried his head on the colonel's thigh.

"Come up here — *closer;*" and putting one arm around Peter's neck he laid the other hand softly on his head, and looked long and tenderly into his eyes. "I've got to leave you, Peter. Don't you feel sorry for me?"

"Oh, Marse Rom!" cried Peter, hiding his face, his whole form shaken by sobs.

"Peter," added the colonel with ineffable gentleness, "if I had served my Master as faithfully as you have served yours, I should not

68

feel ashamed to stand in his presence."

"If my Marseter is ez mussiful
to me ez you have been—"

" I have fixed things so that you
will be comfortable after I am gone.
When your time comes, I should
like you to be laid close to me. We
can take the long sleep together.
Are you willing ?"

" That's whar I want to be laid."

The colonel stretched out his
hand to the vase, and taking the
bunch of pinks, said very calmly:

"Leave these in my hand; I'll
carry them with me." A moment
more, and he added:

"If I shouldn't wake up any
more, good-bye, Peter !"

"Good-bye, Marse Rom !"

And they shook hands a long
time. After this the colonel lay
back on the pillows. His soft, silvery hair contrasted strongly with
his childlike, unspoiled, open face.

69

To the day of his death, as is apt to be true of those who have lived pure lives but never married, he had a boyish strain in him — a softness of nature, showing itself even now in the gentle expression of his mouth. His brown eyes had in them the same boyish look when, just as he was falling asleep, he scarcely opened them to say:

" Pray, Peter."

Peter, on his knees and looking across the colonel's face towards the open door, through which the rays of the rising sun streamed in upon his hoary head, prayed, while the colonel fell asleep, adding a few words for himself now left alone.

Several hours later, memory led the colonel back again through the dim gate-way of the past, and out of that gate-way his spirit finally took flight into the future.

Peter lingered a year. The place went to the colonel's sister, but he was allowed to remain in his quarters. With much thinking of the past, his mind fell into a lightness and a weakness. Sometimes he would be heard crooning the burden of old hymns, or sometimes seen sitting beside the old brass-nailed trunk, fumbling with the spelling-book and *The Pilgrim's Progress.* Often, too, he walked out to the cemetery on the edge of the town, and each time could hardly find the colonel's grave amid the multitude of the dead.

One gusty day in spring, the Scotch sexton, busy with the blades of blue-grass springing from the animated mould, saw his familiar figure standing motionless beside the colonel's resting-place. He had taken off his hat — one of the colonel's last bequests — and laid it on the colonel's head-stone. On his body he wore a strange coat of faded blue, patched and weather-stained, and so moth-eaten that parts of the curious tails had dropped entirely away. In one hand he held an open Bible, and on a much-soiled page he was pointing with his finger to the following words:

" I would not have you ignorant, brethren, concerning them which are asleep."

It would seem that, impelled by love and faith, and guided by his wandering reason, he had come forth to preach his last sermon on the immortality of the soul over the dust of his dead master.

The sexton led him home, and soon afterwards a friend, who had loved them both, laid him beside the colonel.

It was perhaps fitting that his winding-sheet should be the vestment in which, years agone, he had preached to his fellow-slaves in bondage; for if it so be that the dead of this planet shall come forth from their graves clad in the trappings of mortality, then Peter should arise on the Resurrection Day wearing his old jeans coat.

73

THE END

LITTLE BOOKS
BY FAMOUS WRITERS

Uniform with this Volume—with Frontispiece
Fifty Cents a Volume

HARPER & BROTHERS, PUBLISHERS
NEW YORK AND LONDON

☞ *Any of the above works will be sent by mail, postage prepaid, to any part of the United States, Canada, or Mexico, on receipt of the price.*

www.ingramcontent.com/pod-product-compliance
Lightning Source LLC
Chambersburg PA
CBHW030008030726

47499CB00008B/2960